# Fine

# Feathered

# Friend

# Jamila Gavin

Illustrated by
# Dan Williams

# Yellow Bananas

*For Kamala and Vinod*
*J.G.*


*For my niece Nina*
*D.W.*

# Chapter One

RAJU WAS ANGRY. He was so angry he thought he would burst.

'I hate Ma, I hate Pa, I hate Sonia.' Sonia was his elder sister.

'I hate my aunt and my uncle and I hate the world.'

What had brought about all this hate? It was because Raju's mother, father and sister, Sonia, had all gone off to England to attend a wedding and left him behind. Worse than that, instead of leaving him in Bombay where he lived, they had packed him off to the country for two whole months of the summer holidays, to stay with his boring aunt and uncle. They didn't even have any children, and they lived in a boring little village miles from anywhere.

'I'll die of boredom,' Raju had moaned to his best friend Arjun.

Raju was a city boy. He had been born and bred in Bombay. His playground was the city

Fine

Feathered

Friend

This edition first published in Great Britain 2001
By Egmont Children's Books Limited
First published in Great Britain 1996
by Heinemann Young Books,
an imprint of Egmont Children's Books Limited
a division of Egmont Holding Limited
239 Kensington High Street, London W8 6SA
Published in hardback by Heinemann Library,
a division of Reed Educational and Professional Publishing Limited,
by arrangement with Egmont Children's Books Limited.
Text copyright © Jamila Gavin 1996
Illustrations copyright © Dan Williams 2001
The author and illustrator have asserted their moral rights
Paperback ISBN 0 7497 4224 0
Hardback ISBN 0431 06174 2
1 3 5 7 9 10 8 6 4 2
A CIP catalogue record for this title is available from the British Library.
Printed and bound in the U.A.E.

streets and alleyways, the crowded bazaars and the glittering, modern shopping arcades. When he got bored with that, he went to Crawford market. There the great fat merchants sat on the tops of mountains of fruit and vegetables and sweets and spices and every possible kind of edible thing, yelling and shouting their wares.

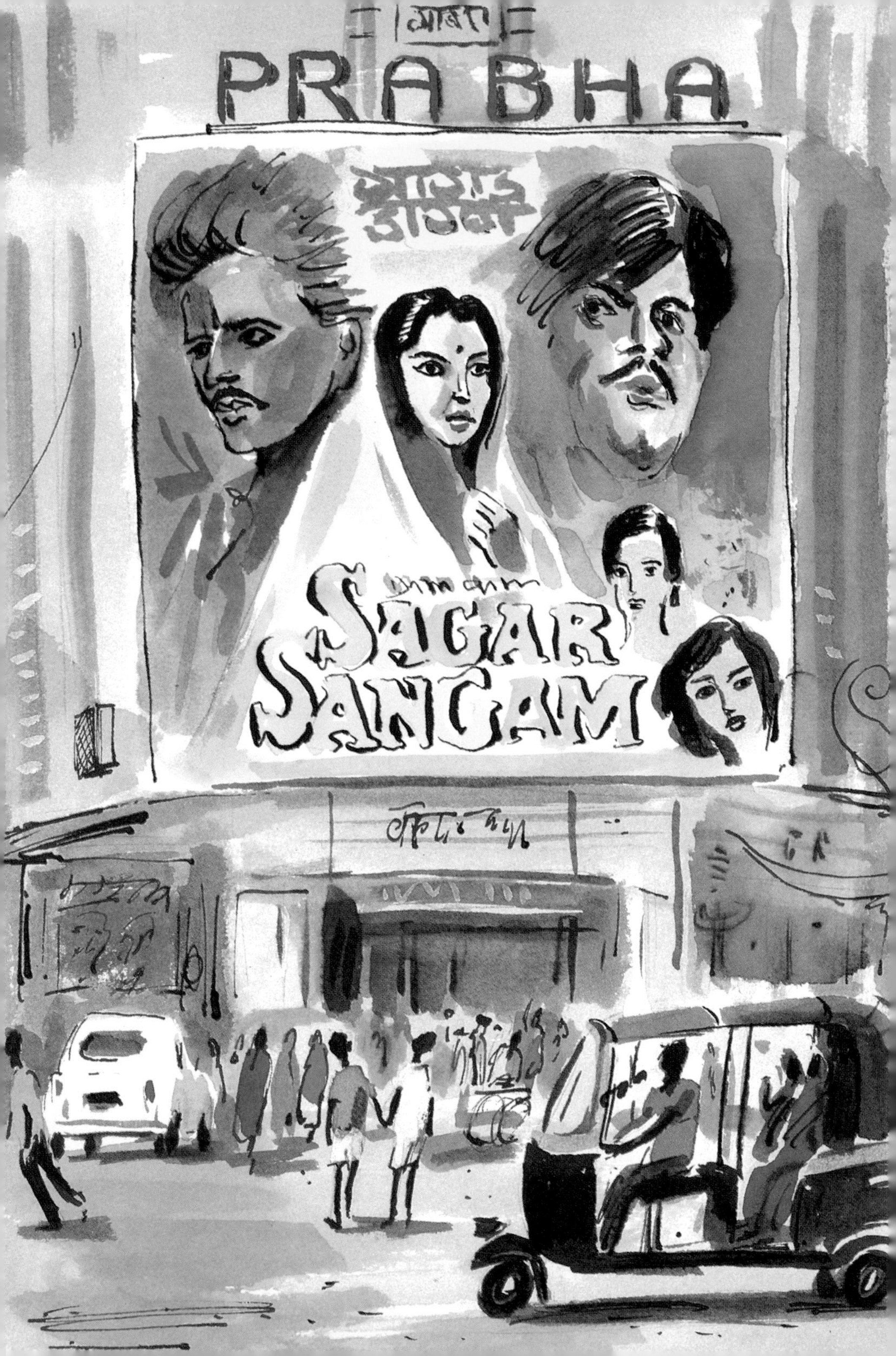
PRABHA
SAGAR
SANGAM

Or he went with his friends to the glitzy cinemas to see the latest films – giggling at the pin-up girls and looking to grow up to be like their dashing, mustachioed heroes. If they had seen all the movies (some of them twice), there was always cricket on the green, swimming in the sea or swaggering into the tearooms of the big hotels to order milkshakes and lemonades.

Now here he was, away from all that. Instead of the bustle of crowds, the honking of traffic and the bright lights of the city, he was in a quiet rural village. Here the loudest sound was the crowing of the cockerel and most people went about on foot or in bullock carts.

The silence disturbed him. 'I hate it, I hate it, I hate it,' he stormed.

He would have run away. He had suggested it to Arjun before he left. 'We could sleep on the beach and scavenge food in the market. We could have real adventures!' His eyes glowed excitedly. But Arjun had told him that he and his family were leaving Bombay too and going to a hill station for the summer. He seemed rather pleased about it. Raju didn't want to run away by himself, so there was no way out. He would just have to stay on the farm and put up it with it. He was stuck with it.

'I do hope you'll make the most of it,' his mother had said cheerfully when she saw Raju's gloomy expression. 'I used to love it when I was a girl. We had such fun with all the animals.'

'Animals?' Raju had exclaimed scornfully. 'Do you call chickens animals?' He knew that it was a chicken farm he was going to.

So while the rest of his family had driven to the airport and boarded a sleek shining aeroplane, Raju had got on to one of those dusty, crowded, long-distance buses, which rattled and shook every bone in your body. For four hours he had bounced along winding roads, up into hills and down on to plains, until at last he reached the little town nearest to his aunt and uncle's farm.

# Chapter Two

THERE THEY WERE, waiting for him at the bus stop, their kindly faces full of smiles. They were so pleased to have their young nephew to stay. Being so far out, they didn't often get to see other members of the family and when you work on a farm, you can't just take a day off when you feel like it.

They told Raju their farm was about three miles away, so Raju thought they would go in a taxi or a car, but his aunt had said enthusiastically, 'I don't suppose you've ever ridden in a bullock cart.'

Raju agreed he hadn't, but neither had he ever wanted to. His great passion was riding in fast cars, whenever he got the opportunity.

'We thought you would enjoy driving the bullock cart! The days have gone when bullocks, camels and elephants were used to bring the produce into the city from the countryside. Now it's all fast, noisy trucks,' his uncle had said with a note of regret in his voice. 'A bullock cart should be quite a novelty for you!'

'Yes,' Raju had answered in a listless voice. He didn't show any interest at all as his uncle tossed his suitcase into the rough wooden cart.

The cart was yoked to a pair of gleaming white, high-humped bullocks, with long, curved, sharp horns which arched over their heads. The horns

were painted bright red and bright blue. Raju couldn't help admiring them, but he kept his thoughts a secret. He was still angry and wanted everyone to know it.

# Chapter Three

'WHO SHALL I play with?' he demanded when they arrived at the farm.

His aunt and uncle looked at each other with raised eyebrows. 'Well, er . . . we thought you might like to help out on the farm. No one really plays here. Even the littlest children have jobs to do, like herding the goats, cleaning out the cowsheds or driving the bullock carts to and from town – that's the job we thought you would enjoy,' said Uncle.

'And of course, there are always the chickens to be attended to. Their feeding gulleys have to be filled, their water-courses kept topped up and plenty of sawdust scattered in the chicken run.'

Raju looked appalled. This was supposed to be his summer holiday, and here they were suggesting that he do all this messy work. 'Chickens! I ask you!' he wrote to Arjun the

next day. 'I wish you were here with me. I don't know who will be my friend.'

Raju had thought perhaps Sher, the guard dog, would be his friend. He was a large, dark brown, powerful, muscled dog who had come bounding out to meet them on that first day. But Sher had barked fiercely, revealing a row of sharp, white fangs. He was as fierce as a tiger and a terror to strangers. Raju had jumped back into the cart as the dog had leapt at them, snarling at Raju because he was a newcomer.

Raju felt ashamed that he had shown fear, but his aunt had said, 'Sher has to be fierce to keep away robbers. Sometimes we get chicken thieves, who come in the night and steal our hens! Sher is a good guard dog. Ever since we got him the robbers have stayed away.' Raju could see why and stayed away from him too.

Perhaps Muni would be a better friend. Muni was a much older dog, but she was nearly blind and spent most of her time asleep, so Raju soon lost interest in her.

He tried to make friends with a pet squirrel called Nipper. Nipper loved scampering across your shoulders and nipping your ear. Raju spent hours holding out his hand and trying to persuade Nipper to come to him, but Nipper preferred Uncle and rejected all Raju's efforts.

So Raju scowled even more. 'There's no one to play with and nothing to do,' he grumbled.

His aunt and uncle sighed. Raju seemed determined not to be happy. It looked as though the next two months were going to be hard, trying to keep their nephew amused.

Then one day, soon after lunch, when hardly anyone was about and his aunt and uncle were resting through the afternoon heat, Raju went into the garden. He sulked around, slashing the bushes with a stick, hating with every muscle in his body.

'I've got nothing to do!' he wailed. The hens and ducks who pecked and softly clucked in the grass, scuttled from beneath his stomping feet.

He felt mean. He wanted to bully something. He saw Queenie, his aunt's favourite shining black hen, half-hidden in the long grass under the lemon tree. She didn't scuttle away as he walked by, so he thrashed his stick at her. How gleeful he felt when she gave a pathetic squawk and heaved herself into the bushes.

That's when Raju saw the egg. He stared at it with faint surprise. He had only ever seen an egg in the market or in his mother's kitchen.

What was an egg doing
out here in the garden?
He picked it up. It
was warm with bits
of feathers stuck
to it. He slowly
realised that it must
be Queenie's egg.
She had been sitting

on it, and he had chased her away.
He felt a pang of guilt, but thought, 'Oh, well,
she's left it now, and finders keepers,' and he
popped it in his pocket.

For a while, he just roamed around, looking at
nothing in particular. His hand was in his pocket,
cradling the egg. Its delicate, oval shape and
extraordinary fragility, gave him an unexpected
tremor of excitement. He forgot about feeling
angry. All he could think about was the egg in
his pocket. He wondered if there was a chick
inside it. He held it protectively, keeping it warm
and safe.

# Chapter Four

THAT NIGHT, HE cocooned the egg in straw and placed it under the warmth of his bedside light, which he decided to leave on, and then went to sleep.

*Tap, tap, tap, crick, crick, crick.* It was only a small pipping sound, but persistent, and it pipped its way into Raju's dream.

*Tap, tap, tap, crick, crick, crick.* Raju woke up. He looked at the egg beneath his bedside lamp. It looked like a small planet, glowing in the black space of night all around. *Tap, tap, tap* . . . the pipping sound got louder, then . . . *CRACK!* The perfect, oval white shell fractured.

Raju sat bolt upright in amazement. A little beak hammered away and burst through the shell. Then, before his very eyes, a dank, lank, scrawny little creature stepped out into the world as bold as brass, cheeping away for all it was worth.

For a moment, Raju was almost afraid. He had seen many strange and wonderful things in Bombay. He had seen snake-charmers draped in writhing pythons; monkeys who danced and turned cartwheels; he had seen magnificent elephants and camels and bears; he had even seen a tiger once, when he was taken to a jungle. But somehow he had never seen anything so magical as a simple white egg breaking open, and a living creature stepping out into the world.

Raju watched it with wonder. It was so small. Beneath the warmth of his bedside lamp, it shook itself and stretched its tiny wings. Soon, the wetness dried, and as it dried, the chick began to fluff up all softly grey with yellow splodges.

Raju's hand closed over the creature and he lifted it on to his palm.

He could feel its heart thudding inside its quivering body, and its dark eyes glistened like glass beads. He held it to his cheek. It was so soft. He looked at it again, standing in the palm of his hand, and it was as though he held creation itself.

He lay back on his pillow, holding the creature to his chest and fell asleep again.

The next morning at breakfast, Raju's aunt and uncle looked at him in amazement. He had a smile on his face. They hadn't seen him smile since the day he came.

'You're looking mighty pleased with yourself today,' commented Uncle.

'Like the cat who got the cream,' agreed his aunt.

Then they heard a funny cheeping coming from somewhere. 'What's that?'

Raju reached into his shirt pocket and pulled out his little chick. 'I found this egg in the bushes yesterday. I kept it warm, first in my pocket then under my bedside lamp, and look – it hatched!' He proudly opened his hand and showed them the little grey chick, shaking and fluffing up its feathers and squawking for food.

'Well I never did!' exclaimed Uncle with a laugh. 'You're a fine one to be sure!' And Raju didn't know if his uncle meant him or the chicken.

'It must be one of Queenie's chicks,' exclaimed his aunt. 'How careless of her to leave it lying around!'

'I suppose I'd better give it back to its mother,' murmured Raju, guiltily remembering how he had frightened Queenie away.

'You can't do that, my boy!' cried his aunt, shaking her head. 'Queenie won't take this chick back. Not now that it's been in your pocket and in your hand. She won't recognise it any more. No, Raju, you hatched the chick. You're its mother now.'

Raju laughed at the thought. 'That's silly. Of course I'm not its mother.'

'The chicken thinks so. The chicken will think it looks like you because you were the first thing it saw when it hatched. We once had a chicken who thought it was a dog because it hatched in the dog basket while the dog was in it. So I hope you will be a responsible parent!'

Raju popped the chicken on to the table in front of him and looked at it with amazement.

The chicken gazed back with its beady eyes.
Then it began cheeping hungrily, scratching
with its pink, four-clawed feet and pecking at
the breadcrumbs on the tablecloth.

Raju's aunt poured some water on to a saucer.
'Make sure it always has plenty to drink,' she
said.

So the chicken who thought it was a boy
stayed with Raju, going everywhere with him.
Instead of joining all the other chickens in the
yard, it insisted on sticking as close to Raju as it
could. Raju didn't mind. He gave his chicken a

name – Pitchou – and spent hours cuddling it and chatting to it while he made sure it was fed and watered and looked after.

It pecked from his plate, and perched on the bath while he bathed, and slept on his bed. And when Raju went out, he carried it with him in his shirt pocket wherever he went. Raju and the chick were inseparable. No one ever saw one without the other.

'One thing you should know,' Raju told it as he put it to bed one night, 'I'm not your mother, but I am your friend. Your very, very best friend.'

# Chapter Five

IT WAS AMAZING how fast the little chick grew. Day by day by day, it got bigger and bigger. Its soft, grey downy feathers darkened and a bright red comb began to grow on its head. Raju realised that his chick was a female.

Soon she was too big to fit in his pocket, so she rode on his shoulder or strutted after him on her thin, peachy legs, never letting Raju out of her sight.

If Raju cycled down the long road to the
bazaar, Pitchou came too, riding proudly in the
front basket, her shiny head swivelling round
as if she were the guide. If Raju rode on the
bullock cart across the fields to the village, so
did Pitchou. She even got into Uncle's car when
they all went for a drive to visit friends.

Now that Raju had a friend, he became so
much happier. He smiled a lot, and didn't mind
helping in the garden. He fed the hens and
checked the hen-sheds each day for eggs. Of
course, Pitchou went with him and sometimes
got muddled up with all the other chickens,
but she always came running as soon as Raju
called her.

Raju couldn't believe it when he realised that two months had passed. Suddenly it was time for him to go home. His bags were packed and his aunt piled him up with baskets of eggs and honey and fresh vegetables and spices to take back to Bombay. Waiting patiently nearby was Pitchou.

'Wherever Raju goes, I go,' her puffed up feathers announced.

Aunt and Uncle drove Raju to the bus station, and there they put him on the bus and made sure that all his luggage was safely tied on to the roof.

'What about that?' asked the bus driver, pointing at the chicken.

'That's my friend,' said Raju. 'She comes with me,' and he carried Pitchou on to the bus. Gently he held her close to him all the time during the long journey back to Bombay.

# Chapter Six

RAJU'S MOTHER AND father and his sister, Sonia, were so excited to see him. They were bursting to tell him all about their trip to England. But Raju was just as excited to tell them all about his pet, Pitchou. His mother looked dubiously at Pitchou. 'You're not really thinking of keeping that chicken here, are you, Raju?' she said.

'That's not just a chicken,' explained Raju. 'Pitchou thinks I'm her mother. She's got to stay with me.'

'But are you sure that a chicken will like living in a Bombay apartment, four floors up, rather than in a country garden?' murmured Father.

'Pitchou wants to be with *me*. She's never left my side since the day she hatched,' insisted Raju.

So Pitchou stayed. Somehow, though, it wasn't like being in Aunt's garden. Fluff and feathers and droppings soon scattered all over the flat and when she fluttered around, she crashed into the television, or knocked over the ornaments. She messed all over the chairs and sofas and she didn't seem to realise that the carpet wasn't the earth. She scraped and dug into it with her sharp claws, tossing up shreds of wool. And she flew up into the curtains as if they were trees.

'It's no good,' sighed Mother finally. 'Either that chicken goes into the pot or back to the country.'

Raju glared at his mother as if she were a murderer. 'Into the pot? How could you even think such a thing?' he howled. 'Eating my chicken would be like cannibalism!'

'Well then, it's back to the farm,' declared Mother. Father agreed. Raju held his beloved hen in his arms. 'But Pitchou thinks I'm her mother. She'll miss me. She'll be miserable.'

'Did you miss me all the time I was away?' demanded Raju's mother.

'Yes!' cried Raju. 'Well . . . ' he added warily, 'not all the time. Only at first.'

'Well then, it will be the same for Pitchou. She'll miss you at first, and then she'll adjust. After all, she's not a chick any more.'

They all looked at the large, sleek, coal-black hen, with her shining feathers and an arch of bright red glowing on her head. 'It's time she had friends of her own kind,' said Mother.

# Chapter Seven

IT WAS A miserable journey back to the country. Raju held his pet – his child – his friend – on his lap all the way back.

The only thing which comforted Raju, was that his aunt and uncle promised that Pitchou would always be his.

'You will promise not to eat her?' pleaded Raju.

'Of course we won't. Come here for your next holidays, and she'll be waiting for you.'

Sadly, Raju said 'Goodbye' to Pitchou. He could hardly bear to watch her bobbing frantically in the basket. She flapped her wings trying desperately to escape and follow Raju back to the car.

Another three months passed before Raju was able to return to the farm. But at last the holidays came, and once more, Raju got on the bone-shaking bus and bounced and rattled all the way to the village. His aunt and uncle were there to meet him with the bullock cart. 'Is Pitchou all right?' he asked them anxiously.

'Yes, she is fine,' they told him, 'but I think you'll find she's changed rather a lot.'

When they arrived at the farm, Sher came rushing out barking and showing his fangs. But this time his tail was wagging because Raju was no longer a stranger. 'Hello Sher!' cried Raju giving him a hug. But all Raju wanted to do was rush off in search of Pitchou.

'She's over in the big yard with the full grown hens,' his aunt told him.

'Which one is she?' Raju looked and looked, calling out Pitchou's name and holding out his hand as he always used to. But when one chicken came towards him, so did another and another, and it was impossible to know which was his.

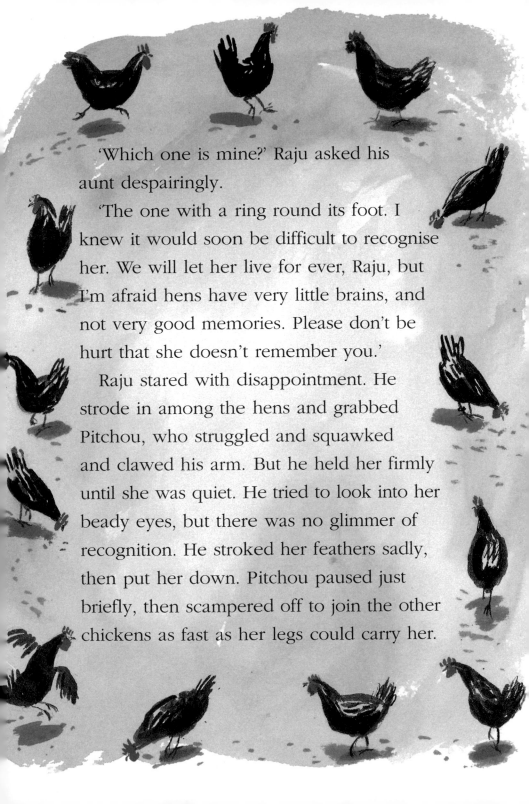

'Which one is mine?' Raju asked his aunt despairingly.

'The one with a ring round its foot. I knew it would soon be difficult to recognise her. We will let her live for ever, Raju, but I'm afraid hens have very little brains, and not very good memories. Please don't be hurt that she doesn't remember you.'

Raju stared with disappointment. He strode in among the hens and grabbed Pitchou, who struggled and squawked and clawed his arm. But he held her firmly until she was quiet. He tried to look into her beady eyes, but there was no glimmer of recognition. He stroked her feathers sadly, then put her down. Pitchou paused just briefly, then scampered off to join the other chickens as fast as her legs could carry her.

'How could you forget me so soon? After all I am your mother,' sighed Raju. He walked down the length of the garden, carefully avoiding the hens and ducks who pecked and clucked in the sunshine. Deep in the shady, long grass beneath the lemon tree, he caught a glimpse of Queenie's shining black feathers. She sat perfectly still and didn't move as he drew near.

Raju smiled. Queenie was broody again. But this time, he wouldn't chase her away.

Suddenly, he felt a warm wet tongue lick his hand. It was old Muni giving him a friendly nudge of recognition. 'Hello, Muni,' said Raju and gave her a hug. As he went back to the house, Sher came rushing towards him with a stick in his mouth. He dropped it at Raju's feet. 'Oh! So you want to play, do you?' he laughed, and threw the stick as far as he could. Sher bounded off and brought it back to Raju again and again.

That evening, Nipper, who had been sitting on Uncle's shoulder nibbling his ear, suddenly leapt across on to Raju's back. 'Well I never!' exclaimed Uncle. 'He's never gone to anyone else but me before.'

Raju smiled happily. 'I like coming here now,' he wrote to his friend Arjun. Somehow, he felt he owed it all to Pitchou.